Marsh Island

Sonya Spreen Bates

Illustrated by
Kasia Charko

ORCA BOOK PUBLISHERS

Library and Archives Canada Cataloguing in Publication

Bates, Sonya Spreen, 1963–
Marsh Island / written by Sonya Spreen Bates; illustrated by Kasia Charko.

(Orca echoes)

ISBN 978-1-55469-117-3

1. Wilderness survival--Juvenile fiction.
I. Charko, Kasia, 1949- II. Title. III. Series: Orca echoes

PS8603.A846M37 2009   jC813'.6   C2008-908029-7

First published in the United States, 2009
Library of Congress Control Number: 2008943124

For my mom, who loved the woods.

Chapter One

EXPLORING

Jake crouched under the giant tree. It felt rough and scratchy on his hand. The smell of the bark made his nose sting. He'd never been in the woods before. There were hundreds and thousands of trees, and no one around but him. He could be anything he wanted to be in these woods.

I'm a panther, thought Jake. *Sleek, black and dangerous. I slink through the grass. My paws are silent on the jungle floor. My eyes dart through the trees. I hear the crack of a twig, see movement in the shadows. I spot my prey.*

"Jake? Jake?" It was Jake's brother Tommy, making as much noise as a T. rex. The racket would scare off

1

prey for miles. Jake spun around. *A hunter!* he thought. *I won't let him capture me.* He crouched lower and crept behind a tree trunk.

"Jake, come out!" called Tommy. "This isn't funny." His voice wobbled.

Jake tilted his head up and sniffed. *I smell fear*, he thought.

Tommy's stumbling footsteps moved closer. "Dad won't like this," he said to the forest around him. "We're supposed to stay near the tent."

Jake scowled. Tommy was such a spoilsport. Jake had wanted to leave him at home. This was Jake's first camping trip, and he'd wanted it to be special. He was nine now, and he had wanted to spend some time alone with Dad. But Tommy had whined and complained, and Dad had let him come.

Marsh Island was no place for Tommy. Tommy was only seven. He didn't like bugs, he didn't like tents and he didn't like noises in the night. There were plenty of noises on Marsh Island. Even Jake had lain awake the first couple of nights, listening to the strange sounds of the forest.

I wait, thought Jake. *He comes closer. A few more steps…wait for it…*

"Jake?"

With a mighty roar, Jake jumped out from behind the tree.

Tommy screamed.

Jake fell to the ground, laughing.

"You—you—," Tommy choked out.

"You should have seen your face!" said Jake.

"Yeah? Well, it's not funny," shouted Tommy, his face like a thundercloud. Tommy's curly brown hair sprang up wildly around his head. And in his new green T-shirt and shorts, he looked like an angry little elf.

Jake wiped the tears off his face with his shirt. "That's what you think," he said, getting to his feet.

It was probably the funniest thing he'd ever seen. Except for the time Tommy got his head stuck between the bars of the lion cage at the zoo. Tommy had freaked.

Jake wiped his dirty hands on his shorts and pushed his hair off his face. He had brown hair like Tommy's, but it was dead straight. It always seemed to get in his eyes.

They were deep in the woods. The trail wound through the forest and curved out of sight. Behind them was the tent, nestled in the trees like a bright blue flower in a vegetable patch. If he looked closely, Jake could see Dad's red-checkered shirt through the tent's open flap.

"I'm going back," said Tommy.

Jake shrugged. "Do what you like. But you know what Dad will say if you wake him up, and I'm not coming with you. I'm not spending all week sitting around a campfire eating burned marshmallows."

"I like marshmallows," said Tommy, stubbornly.

Jake shook his head and started down the trail. He knew Tommy would follow. He'd never be brave enough to go back to the campsite alone.

The trail wasn't very wide. Jake had to push branches out of the way as he walked. *It's probably an animal trail*, he thought. *Maybe a deer track.* Before long he lost sight of the tent. *Maybe I should have brought the compass Grandpa gave me*, he thought. But he didn't want to go back. Dad hadn't taken them any farther than the beach, and he was dying to explore. Besides, going back would be giving in. And there's no way he'd give in to Tommy.

"Wait! Wait for me!" cried Tommy, rushing to catch up.

Jake smirked. "Wuss," he muttered under his breath.

Jake led the way down the trail. He kept the tent at his back and moved toward the sun. It was cool under the trees, and the smell of the forest tickled his nose.

It was a strange smell, kind of like the dirt in the garden after his mom had dug in the compost. A couple of little gray warblers swooped from branch to branch overhead.

Jake wasn't into birds. There were plenty of them at home. Dad built birdfeeders and filled them with seeds and honey to attract all sorts of birds. The garden was full of them. No, Jake was hoping to see something new, something wild. A rabbit maybe, or even a fox. But Tommy was puffing like a buffalo. Not much chance of sneaking up on something with him around.

Jake scowled over his shoulder at Tommy to shush him. Here he was, spoiling his fun again. It was just like last year, when Dad took them go-carting. Tommy had putted around the course so slowly. After only one circuit, all the other go-carts were lined up behind him. No one could get past because Tommy was such a hopeless driver.

It wasn't Jake's fault Tommy had crashed. It's not like Jake hadn't warned him. He'd yelled at Tommy to get out of the way. But when Jake had tried to sneak past, Tommy panicked and drove straight into the wall. How stupid was that? Then he'd made such a fuss that Dad dragged Jake off the course and they all went home. A pain, that's what Tommy was.

Jake stopped for a moment and looked around. The trail was starting to climb. *If it goes right up to the top of the mountain*, he thought, *we could see all the way out to sea.* He listened. He could hear water running off to his left. Was it a creek or a waterfall? He stepped off the trail and pushed through the bushes. He followed the sound until he found a wide stream, bubbling over the rocks.

"Cool," he said. *I bet we'll find some frogs*, he thought, *or maybe some fish.*

Tommy tugged at his shirt. "Let's go back now," he said.

"Not yet," said Jake, shaking him off. "I want to have a look around." He stepped onto a boulder at the stream's edge.

I'm an explorer, thought Jake. *My feet are the first to cross this water and step onto new land.*

He held his head high and leaped across to another rock. But the stone was wet and slippery. Before he could say *Christopher Columbus*, his foot plunged into the stream. The water was like ice. He sucked in his breath and hopped across the stream to a rock on the other side.

"Where are you going, Jake?" called Tommy. "Aren't we going back?"

Jake ignored him.

New land, he thought. *Untouched by humans. The only footprints here will be animal tracks. Frogs, birds, foxes, deer, maybe even bears!* His heart beat a little faster at the thought, and he had a quick look around. Then he laughed at himself. There weren't any bears around here.

But something had been there. Halfway up the bank, he spotted a dark shape under a bush. He stepped off the rock and headed toward it, his shoes sinking into the soft muddy bank.

"Jake? Come back," said Tommy. His voice was wobbling again.

"In a minute," called Jake. "I found something."

Chapter Two

BURIED TREASURE

Jake shoved the bush out of the way and knelt to have a closer look. Two sticks were stuck in the ground and crossed at the middle to make an X.

"What is it? What did you find?" asked Tommy, splashing across the stream. He clambered up the bank and dropped to his knees next to Jake.

"I'm not sure," said Jake. "But someone put these sticks here on purpose. You know, so they could find the spot again."

"Like pirate treasure? X marks the spot?"

"Yeah." Jake grinned. "Come on, help me dig."

Jake pulled out the two sticks. He gave one to Tommy.

I am a pirate, Jake thought, *returning for my buried treasure. Gold, coins, jewels, all mine.* He scraped away at the dirt, punching the stick into the mud. *Could a pirate really have buried something here?* he wondered. Then he remembered something his dad had told him the night before they'd left home. A tale about the island, about some madman who'd lived there, years and years ago. He'd thought it was just a story, but maybe it was true.

"I wonder if crazy old Marsh put these here," he said.

"Who?"

"Didn't Dad tell you the Marsh Island story?"

"No." Tommy sniffed and wiped his nose on his sleeve.

"Well, the island was named after this man, Alfred Marsh," said Jake. He kept digging and didn't look up. "Marsh was rich—I think he owned a bank or something—and lived in this huge mansion in the city. He had heaps of servants waiting on him all day, bringing him whatever he wanted, answering the phone, driving him around. All he had to do was snap his fingers, and someone came running."

Jake held his hand up and clicked his fingers sharply at Tommy. Tommy giggled.

Jake picked a couple of rocks out of the hole and tossed them aside. "But one day the bank went bust, and he went nuts."

"What do you mean?"

"He turned into a zombie. Just lay in bed and stared at the ceiling. Didn't talk, didn't eat, didn't get up."

Tommy stopped digging. "Not even to go to the bathroom?"

"Nah," said Jake, flicking his hair out of his eyes. "They didn't have any servants anymore, so *Mrs.* Marsh had to put diapers on him like a baby."

"Ewww!" Tommy wrinkled his nose.

Jake stabbed his stick in the hole. "Then one day, he got out of bed and walked out the door.

Didn't say anything to anyone, just walked out. He headed straight to the shore, stole a rowboat and rowed out to this island."

"You mean *this* island?"

"Yup, the same one we're standing on. That's why it's called Marsh Island. He disappeared out here, and no one ever saw him again."

"You—you mean he died out here?" asked Tommy, looking over his shoulder.

Suddenly it felt very cold squatting under the bush. Jake glanced into the trees behind them, just like Tommy had. He had a strange feeling, as if he was being watched.

Don't be stupid, Jake thought. *You're imagining things.* He jammed his stick deeper into the dirt.

"Story goes that his wife rowed out and left food for him once in a while. The food always disappeared, but she never saw him again."

Jake's stick hit something hard. His stomach did a flip.

"I found something!" he cried. He threw the stick away and dug with his hands. He clawed at the hole like a dog searching for a lost bone. Dirt ground under his fingernails and hard bits of mud scraped at his skin. Whatever was buried there, it had been there a long, long time. The mud was stuck to it like cement.

"Maybe you should leave it," said Tommy.

Jake scowled at him. "What are you talking about? We've found some treasure, Tommy. Treasure!"

Tommy looked fearfully into the bushes. "Maybe we shouldn't dig it up," he said. "Someone might come back for it."

"Don't be stupid," Jake scoffed. He followed Tommy's gaze into the trees. It was quiet. Almost too quiet. He shook himself and kept digging. "No one's lived on this island for years."

The object in the ground was solid. Jake thought it might be made of wood. "It feels like a box," he said. He scrabbled away a bit more dirt, dug his fingers in under the bottom and pried it loose. The box came out with a *schloop*.

"Cool," Jake said, running his hands across the top. The wood was cold and clammy.

"Do—do you think that crazy guy Marsh buried it here?" asked Tommy.

Jake felt a nervous flutter in his stomach. "Could be. It sure looks old enough." A weird feeling was creeping over him. It felt like hundreds of ants were crawling up his back. "Bet he took his wife's jewelry or something and hid it out here." He turned the box over, looking for the latch. *Could it really have belonged to Alfred Marsh?* he wondered.

Tommy moved closer to Jake and peered into the woods. "Does—does he still live here?" Tommy whispered.

"Alfred Marsh?" Jake laughed. "Get real. That was, like, two hundred years ago. He's long gone. But…" Jake stared into Tommy's eyes and continued in a

low voice, "Some people say he's still wandering the island, looking for his lost fortune."

Tommy's eyes grew big and round.

Suddenly there was a loud *CRACK* in the bushes. Jake's head snapped up. Those branches had definitely moved!

Chapter Three

ESCAPE

Tommy screamed. "It's him!" he shrieked.

"Run for it!" Jake yelled.

Jake leaped to his feet, grabbed the box and dashed into the woods without looking back. He pushed his legs hard and fast, his heart banging against his ribs. Twigs whipped at Jake's face. Roots leaped up to trip him. He couldn't breathe. He glanced back, and a huge shadow lunged out from behind a tree.

"Faster, Tommy!" he yelled.

A boulder appeared in front of him. Jake leaped over it. He dodged around a couple of spruce trees and then plowed through some bushes. The blood pounded in his ears. He didn't care which way he went. He had to get away!

He raced up a hill, lungs screaming for air, and across a gravelly patch at the top. Was Tommy still behind him? He didn't dare look. A cold draft fanned the back of his neck, speeding him on. His legs were killing him, but he made them go faster, around a large moss-covered rock and down a slope, ducking around a tree at the bottom.

He raced up another hill, crossed over an animal trail and plunged back into the woods. He thought he would get away. He thought he'd be fast enough, but he didn't see the log until it was too late. He took a giant leap, tripped, and tumbled headfirst into a pile of leaves.

He lay where he fell, unable to move. His brain screamed at him to get up, keep going, get away. All he could do was lie there and gasp for air. He cowered behind the log, waiting, listening. What had been following him? Was it still there?

Could it see him or hear him…or even smell him? Had he escaped? And what had happened to Tommy?

The woods were quiet. Even the birds were silent. All Jake could hear was himself, panting like an old dog. But as his breathing quieted and his heart slowed, a weird moaning drifted down the trail. He couldn't tell what was making the sound, but it was moving toward him.

He made himself as small as he could, closed his eyes tight and held his breath. Closer and closer came the sound. It was a rasping, groaning sort of noise, low and throaty. Jake bit his lip.

Then a small voice called out. "Jake?"

It was Tommy!

Jake jumped up and put a finger to his lips. "*Ssshhh!*" he hissed. He'd never been so glad to see his brother. He dragged Tommy over the log, pushed him to the ground and peered back over the top. He scanned the path. Nothing stirred. Everything was quiet.

Jake sank into the leaves and wiped the sweat off his face. *That was close*, he thought.

Tommy moaned again. Jake saw that he was shaking. Jake was feeling a bit shaky himself, but he'd never let Tommy know it.

"What was that, Jake?" Tommy asked. "Was it Alf—?"

"No." Jake laughed nervously. "Of course not. It was probably just a bird."

"That wasn't a bird!" said Tommy.

"Well, a—a skunk then, or a raccoon," said Jake. He glanced back at the trail. Nothing moved.

"If that was a skunk, how come you were so scared?"

"You were the one who was screaming like a werewolf was after you," said Jake. "I wasn't scared."

"You were so!" said Tommy.

"Was not!"

"Were too!"

"Wuss!" Jake shouted.

"Double wuss!"

Jake glared at Tommy's bright red face. Little brothers could be such a pain.

"I want to go back to camp," Tommy said.

"All right," Jake said. "But quit screaming."

Jake tried to stand but stumbled over something lying near his feet. It was the box they'd dug up. He must have dropped it when he tripped over the log. Well, he'd brought it this far, he wasn't going to lose it now. He picked it up, tucked it under his arm and looked around to get his bearings, flicking his hair out of his eyes.

Which way should they go? Back to the stream? Just thinking about it made Jake's insides turn to mush. It might not have been Alfred Marsh in those bushes, but *something* had been there. He would have to find another way back.

"Let's go," Tommy whined.

"I'm thinking," Jake said.

He looked around for something to climb. If he could get up high enough to see the tent, they could find a different way back to the campsite. *That big pine tree at the top of the hill might work*, he thought. But he didn't get very far. He'd only taken a couple of steps when he spotted something strange in the bushes. He moved closer and peered through the trees.

"Come on." Tommy tugged at Jake's shirt again.

"Just a minute," said Jake. "There's something in there." He took another couple of steps and shoved a branch out of the way to get a better look. His breath came out in a long low whistle.

"Look at this," he said.

Chapter Four

OLD MAN MARSH

Jake pushed his way through the bushes into a clearing. It wasn't very big, but it was large enough to provide shelter for a small round hut.

"Wow," said Jake. "I bet this was Alfred Marsh's hideout."

The hut was made of sticks and mud and leaned a little to one side. Jake moved closer.

"Let's go," Tommy said, shifting nervously from one foot to the other.

Jake ignored him. "No wonder no one ever found Alfred Marsh. You'd never know this place was here." The ground crunched under Jake's feet.

Clumps of clay and ground shells lay scattered in front of the door.

I've been shipwrecked on a deserted island, he thought. *I built this hut with my bare hands. I live on nuts and berries and creek water. No one knows where I am. No one will ever find me.* A bird whistled, and he glanced back into the trees.

"Don't go in there, Jake," said Tommy.

The walls of the hut were cracked and brittle. Jake reached out and the mud crumbled under his fingers. *How long has this been here?* he wondered.

"I'm just having a look," Jake said. The door was woven together with vines. It hung crookedly over the opening. Jake pulled it open gently, afraid it might fall off the doorframe.

The first thing Jake noticed inside the hut was the smell. He wrinkled his nose. The stale and musty air smelled a bit like smoke. *How long since*

31

anyone has been here, he wondered. *Am I the first person to enter since—?* The door fell closed behind him with a loud *CLUNK*, and Jake jumped.

He laughed at himself, but the butterflies in his stomach wouldn't go away. It was cold and dark. Little slices of light filtered through the cracks in the walls. As his eyes adjusted, he saw a pile of gray ashes on the dirt floor. *Was this from Alfred Marsh's last fire?* he wondered. His scalp started to prickle.

"Come on, Jake!" called Tommy. "This place is giving me the creeps!"

Jake moved farther into the hut and squatted next to the ashes. What would it have been like to live here, alone in the woods? No TV, no videogames, no telephone, not even a toilet. Hunting for food, hauling water from the stream. Who would want to live like that?

Jake shivered. Alfred Marsh, that's who. Alfred Marsh, who had once been a rich and successful man. Alfred Marsh, who had come to this island and never been seen again. A cold draft blew across the back of Jake's neck. He swung around. Had something moved? He heard a scream.

Jake's blood turned cold. He jumped up and dashed out the door. "Tommy!"

Tommy was nowhere in sight.

"Tommy!" Jake called again.

No answer.

Jake shoved his way through the bushes and back to the pile of leaves he'd been sitting on before. He had told Tommy that he wasn't scared. He had yelled at him and called him a wuss. Well, he was scared now.

"Tommy! Where are you?"

"Jake!" Tommy's voice was faint.

Jake barreled through the trees toward it. This was all his fault. Tommy had wanted to go back to the tent, hadn't even wanted to go exploring. But no, Jake had to go snooping around in the hut. If anything happened to him—

"I'm coming, Tommy!" he yelled.

"Help!" The voice was louder. More like a scream than a yell.

Jake ran faster. His chest was so tight he could hardly breathe. He crashed through a bush and fell into a knee-deep pool of water. The stream! In a flash, the cold creepy feeling washed over him again. It was the same feeling he'd had when they dug up the box downstream. He had to find his brother. He plowed through the water and scrambled up the bank.

"Tommy!"

"Jake! Hurry!"

"TOM—" Jake stopped so suddenly he almost swallowed his tongue. He felt like an icicle had stabbed him in the heart.

There was Tommy, backed up against a rock. His face was white, and his eyes were bugged out of his head. But it wasn't the look on Tommy's face that sent a chill through Jake's bones. It was the shadowy figure in the trees, back hunched, arms stretched toward Tommy.

Chapter Five

SPOOKED!

"Leave him alone!" Jake shouted.

The man whirled around. Cold hard eyes bore into him.

Jake froze. Only the hammering in his chest told him that he hadn't turned to ice. *Run!* his mind screamed. But Tommy was trapped against the rocks. He couldn't leave him.

The man took a step forward. He had a dirty gray beard and horrible black teeth.

I am a warrior, Jake told himself. *I am strong and brave. I can protect us.*

Suddenly he remembered the box clutched under his arm. He hurled it at the man's head.

"Run, Tommy!" he screamed.

Tommy sped past, and Jake took off after him. There was a shout, and the sound of heavy footfalls.

Jake ran faster than he'd ever run in his life. His legs pumped like the pistons in a monster truck. "Faster, Tommy!" he urged.

The ground was rough and uneven. Jake stumbled as the ground dipped beneath him. Up ahead, Tommy slipped and fell. Jake thumped down on top of his brother and then scrambled up, pulling Tommy with him. There was a crash behind them.

"Quick! To the top of that hill!" yelled Jake.

They clambered up the hill, half running, half stumbling. Jake glanced back, expecting to see the dirty scowling face of the stranger. Was it Alfred Marsh? *It couldn't be*, his mind told him. But something inside him told him it was.

They sprinted the last few meters to the top, gasping for air.

"We have to find Dad," Jake said. "Look for the tent." His eyes combed the hillside. The tent was down there somewhere, hidden in the trees. They had to find it. It was their only hope.

"I don't see it anywhere," cried Tommy.

"Keep looking!" snapped Jake.

He could feel Tommy close beside him, his body tense. Jake was feeling panicked too. Where was the tent? He heard a shout. The voice was closer than he'd expected.

"It's got to be here. It's got to," he mumbled.

He spotted a small patch of blue.

"There it is!" he shouted. "Come on!" He grabbed Tommy's hand and sped down the slope, ducking around trees and jumping over rocks. Branches grabbed at his shirt and scratched his arms, but he didn't care.

They were almost at the campsite. Dad would be there, and he'd take them home, off this island

and away from whatever was haunting it. Home, where Mom and Grandpa were puttering around in the garden, waiting for them to return, eager to hear about their adventures. Home, where exploring meant a trip downtown on the bus, where he could buy a drink and a hot dog at the corner store. Home, where Alfred Marsh stayed in stories where he belonged.

Jake could see the tent.

"There it is, Tommy! Hurry."

They sprinted toward the campsite.

"Dad! Dad!" they called out.

Jake burst out of the bushes, tripped and fell to the ground. Tommy tumbled down on top of him.

"Jake! Tommy!" Dad helped them to sit up. "Where have you been? I've been worried."

"Dad, you'll never believe it, we—," said Jake.

"There's ghosts here, real live ghosts and—," said Tommy.

Both boys stopped. A shadow moved on the side of the tent.

"Beg your pardon," said a deep voice.

Jake's head jerked up. He saw trousers smeared with mud, a dirty gray beard and dark beady eyes.

Chapter Six

GHOST?

Jake couldn't believe it. They had escaped from the stranger and raced to the campsite. How could the man have made it to the tent so fast? Jake leaped to his feet. "Leave us alone!" he shouted. "Go away! We haven't done anything to you!"

"Jake!" Dad put his hand on Jake's shoulder.

"But Dad, it's—it's—"

"Chris Mumford," said the man. He stepped forward and tipped his hat. "Marsh Island Historical Society."

Dad shook his hand. "Pleased to meet you," he said.

"You mean—you're not Alfred Marsh?" asked Jake.

Dad stared at him. "Jake!"

"Let me explain," said the man, hiding a smile behind his hand. "I came across the boys up at Marsh's Hut. I do a bit of work up there, preserving the historical site. Think I gave them a fright. The young fella here took off so fast I was afraid he'd get lost in the woods. Had to follow him for a bit, till his older brother here found him." He touched the side of his forehead where an angry red lump was forming. "Didn't mean to scare them."

Jake took a closer look at Chris Mumford. He was wearing khaki cargo pants and hiking boots. His beard was gray but flecked with black and neatly trimmed. There was a backpack slung over his shoulder. He smiled at Jake. Mumford's teeth were straight and white. Jake squeezed his eyes shut. How could he have ever thought this was Alfred Marsh?

"Ha!" Jake laughed a fake laugh. "You didn't scare us, not really. We were only fooling. Right, Tommy?"

Tommy didn't say anything.

"Right, Tommy?" Jake gave him a nudge.

"Oh. Yeah," said Tommy, his voice almost a whisper. "Only fooling." He took a step away from the stranger, moving closer to his father.

Chris Mumford smiled. "Well, I'm glad to hear that. I just wanted to make sure you got back okay."

Jake nodded. He felt about as dumb as a slug with a head cold. Alfred Marsh! What had he been thinking?

"We're grateful for your concern," said Dad, putting an arm around Tommy. "They're fine. Nothing a bath and a few Band-Aids won't cure."

"Good, good." Chris Mumford smiled at Jake again and his eyes twinkled. "Oh, and by the way…"

He took off his backpack and rummaged around inside. "I believe this belongs to you."

Jake stared at the dirty wooden box. He remembered the cold, clammy feel of it in his hands, and their race through the woods. He swallowed.

"Uh, yeah, sort of." He looked at Tommy. "We dug it up down by the stream." *It must have been Chris Mumford we heard in the bushes*, he thought. *He was probably trying to stop us from digging up the box.* "Um—I'm sorry about your head." He gestured toward the lump on Chris Mumford's forehead. "And about digging up the box. We didn't know about the Historical Society. We'll put it back, just like it was."

"Oh no you won't," said Chris Mumford.

Jake looked up. The man was smiling!

"We've been looking for Marsh's treasure for years. In fact, there's a reward for its recovery."

Jake couldn't believe his ears. "A reward?"

"Yep, five hundred dollars. And if this box contains what I think it does, that reward is all yours."

Jake grinned. *I could be a hero*, he thought. *Discoverer of the lost treasure of Alfred Marsh. I'll be famous.*

Chris Mumford set the box on the ground and knelt in front of it.

"I've been waiting thirty years to see what's in this box. Let's have a look, shall we?"

Carefully, he pried the lid off the box with his pocketknife, taking care not to damage the wood. Jake held his breath as they all leaned forward to see what was inside.

At first he couldn't see anything. Chris Mumford reached his hand in and drew out a folded piece of paper and a wad of dirty cloth. Unwrapping the cloth, he pulled out a small stone. He whistled softly.

"Do you know what this is?" he said, holding it up.

Jake squinted at it. The stone was about the size of a golf ball, dull and gray, with little red patches all over it. His shoulders drooped. He'd been imagining gold or diamonds or stacks of money or something. Not a hunk of stone that looked as if it belonged in Tommy's rock collection.

Jake shrugged. "It's just a rock," he said.

Chris Mumford shook his head. "If I'm not mistaken, this is no ordinary rock." He unfolded the paper. "Yes, just as I thought."

"What?" said Jake. "What is it?"

Chris Mumford held the stone up high. As the sunlight struck it, the red patches seemed to glow with an inner light. "This," he said, "is the famous Marsh Ruby."

"Marsh Ruby?" said Jake. "As in Alfred Marsh?"

"It is the same family, yes," said Chris Mumford. "Alfred's great-great-great-grandfather, Charles Marsh, discovered this stone in 1754. It was a major discovery of the time. But the stone disappeared a year later and was never seen again. Everyone thought it had been stolen. The family must have been hiding it all this time." He shook his head. "There was a rumor Alfred Marsh brought a family treasure out here to the island. To protect it from the debt collectors. I never imagined it was the Marsh Ruby."

Jake looked at the stone more closely. "What's so special about it? It doesn't look like it's worth very much."

"It just needs some polishing," said Chris Mumford, wrapping it in the cloth and putting it back in the box. "Believe me, this stone is worth plenty. And this letter proves it's genuine." He gestured to the yellowed paper in his hand before placing it carefully next to the stone.

Closing the lid of the box, he tucked it under his arm and slung his pack over his shoulder.

"This is a major find for the Historical Society. Thank you, boys. I'll come back with your reward check tomorrow, and you can show me where the site is." He shook hands with Jake's dad again and turned to go.

"Wait!" Jake called. "You don't need us to show you where we dug up the box. You saw us at the stream…didn't you?"

Chris Mumford looked at him in confusion.

"We heard someone in the bushes. That was you, right?" Jake said.

Chris Mumford shook his head. "No, I've been up at the hut all morning. It was probably just a bird."

"Yeah, a bird," said Jake, glancing at Tommy. He remembered the dark shadow behind the tree and the chill on his neck. Whatever it was, it definitely hadn't been a bird.

Chris Mumford winked at him. "Don't worry, you're not the first person to think they've seen Alfred Marsh on this island. But I've been working for the Historical Society for a long time. There's nothing spookier here than a few bats in Smuggler's Cave."

"Smuggler's Cave?" said Jake. "What's that?"

The man smiled and scratched his beard. "Well, that's a story for another day," he said. He raised a hand in salute and disappeared into the trees.

"Sounds like you two have had quite a morning," said Dad, clamping a hand on Jake's shoulder. "Do you still think camping is dull?"

Jake peered down the trail after Chris Mumford. The woods were quiet. The man had left as silently as he'd come.

"No, this island is definitely *not* dull," Jake said. He looked over at Tommy and winked. "But, if you don't mind, I think we'll hang out around camp for a while."

Tommy's face broke into a grin. He tried to wink back, but he looked like an orangutan with a toothache.

Jake laughed. Brothers could be such a pain. He threw his arm around Tommy and ruffled his hair. "How about we roast some marshmallows?" he said.

Sonya Spreen Bates is a Canadian writer living in Australia. As a child, when she wasn't riding horses, she loved to read and daydream and scribble down short stories that she never dared to show anyone. As well as being a writer and a mom, Sonya also works with children with communication disorders. *Marsh Island* is her first book with Orca.